Anita Mulvey had always dreamed of being a writer although it wasn't until something strange happened that she was finally able to begin writing in earnest. In April 2018, Anita suddenly went blind and eventually retired from primary school teaching, a job she loved. But this unexpected event enabled her to embark on her journey to become an author. Anita says that positive outcomes can occur even when we are faced with adversity – never give up hope!

Born and raised in Aldershot, Hampshire, Anita now lives very happily on the wonderful Isle of Man.

Dedicated to my fabulous family.

Anita Mulvey

DRAGON TIMES

AUSTIN MACAULEY PUBLISHERS™
LONDON · CAMBRIDGE · NEW YORK · SHARJAH

A CIP catalogue record for this title is available from the British Library.

ISBN 9781398446304 (Paperback)
ISBN 9781398446311 (Hardback)
ISBN 9781398446335 (ePub e-book)
ISBN 9781398446328 (Audiobook)

www.austinmacauley.com

First Published 2022
Austin Macauley Publishers Ltd®
1 Canada Square
Canary Wharf
London
E14 5AA

Manx Blind Welfare for their support, technology and training.

RNIB for their support and training, helping me to adapt to my new blindness.

All the fabulous staff at St Paul's Eye Hospital, Liverpool, for all their marvellous support and care at a very difficult stage in my life.

My partner, friends, and family for everything!!!

A special mention to thank my mum, Sandra, for her proofreading, research, and super suggestions.

All the children I have ever taught – you taught me so much too!

Finally, all the wonderful people at Austin Macauley who have helped me to fulfil my dreams.

Have you ever wondered if dragons are real?

Siblings Lily and Alexander thought that dragons exist only in stories. But they were wrong!

In extraordinary times, extraordinary things can happen.

Prologue - Part 1

"Have you ever seen a dragon?"

"No? What's that? What are you saying? Dragons aren't real?"

"Well of course they're real. Just because you haven't seen one, it doesn't mean that dragons don't exist!"

The sad truth is that there are not many left nowadays. In times gone by, we humans lived very happily with dragons by our sides. But times change; nothing stays the same forever.

Long, long ago people had real fires to heat their homes and to do their cooking on; and curled up contentedly in front of most fireplaces, were dragons.

It was a perfect arrangement on both sides. Who better to light your fire than a tame dragon? And the easiest way to keep a dragon happy is to ask him or her to breathe out flames for you, and then let them snooze in the warmth from your fireplace.

But times, as we've already said, change. Many changes are great and most humans now enjoy central heating in their homes and who can blame them? No more chopping logs; no more messy coal; no more hearths to sweep, ash to clear away or fire grates to blacken. All we have to do now is flick a switch or two and your whole house warms up in a jiffy.

It is a strange fact that lots of us still have a rug by our fireplaces, even though they are no longer needed to make dragons as comfortable as possible. Sadly, our hearth-side rugs are quite empty of dragons.

But what has happened to all the dragons? Oh yes, there are still a few people without central heating and you might be lucky enough to see their dragons. However, most of us don't need dragons any more. In fact, they are now so rare that people have forgotten all about dragons and believe them to exist only in stories or be the result of overwrought imaginations.

But if you are clever and know where to look, you just might be fortunate enough to meet a real dragon. Good luck!

Prologue - Part 2
Where Do Dragons Live?

Most dragons live in caves, especially the sort of caves you find in mountains. So if you are determined to find a dragon, head to your nearest mountain and search all the caves you can. Dragons particularly enjoy remote locations, so the further away from busy towns and cities they are, the happier they will be and your chances of meeting one of these rare creatures will be higher.

Another good place to look is a castle. Oh no, not the sort of castle with a shop and a cafe, tour guides and those red, velvety ropes that keep visitors out of the most interesting parts.

No, the sort of castle where a dragon might live is a tumble-down place with crumbling walls and spiral staircases leading up to towers which fell down centuries ago.

It doesn't even have to be a great big castle. Just like us humans, dragons come in all different shapes and sizes. So a small place may not look too promising to house a large dragon, but could make a perfect home for a small one.

You just never know when you might be lucky enough to meet a dragon. You could search for years and years and years and *still* never find a real, live dragon.

Or you might not even be looking for one at all. Some people simply stumble upon a dragon, quite by chance.

You just never know!

Chapter 1

It started out as an ordinary day, but it didn't finish that way; quite the opposite, in fact. We are living in strange times, *very* strange times.

Alexander and Lily got up as usual, had breakfast, got ready as usual and then went to school, as usual. Most of the day went along as it normally did and then it all changed.

Everyone filed into the hall for an extra assembly. There was a buzz of excitement as all the children wondered what was happening. The teachers were all looking quite solemn.

What on Earth was going on?

The head teacher, Mr Latimer, stood at the front of the hall and made a startling announcement:

"Our school is going to shut today!"

There was a stunned silence for a moment, then a few gasps and murmurs of surprise. Then lots of children started talking all at once, full of questions. There were even one or two little cheers.

Mr Latimer held up one hand, rather like a police officer directing traffic, and waited until the hall was silent once more.

"You have all heard the news by now, I expect," he said. "There is a dreadful virus sweeping round our country – round the whole world, in fact. To keep you all safe, the government has decided to close most schools."

Again, he held up his hand and waited for the children to settle down and listen.

"Most of you will stay at home with your parents," continued Mr Latimer. "Many of your parents' places of work will also be shut, so you can stay safe at home together. It is very important that we all stay home as much as possible to stop the virus from spreading. It's being called a 'lockdown' but try not to worry. We won't be literally locked in, but as I said, we must all stay home as much as we can to stop the spread of this virus."

There was another buzz of excitement at these words and the head teacher was wise enough to wait for a few minutes to let the hubbub subside before he continued.

"Your teachers will give you extra homework today and they will be posting activities online for all of you who are lucky enough to have internet access at home. Remember to take all your things home today – coats, lunchboxes, pencil cases, PE kits and so on," he said.

"These children please stay behind in the hall as we are making special arrangements for you." Mr Latimer proceeded to read out a short list of names, including Lily and Alexander. They waited anxiously. What on Earth was he going to say next?

Well, the head teacher explained that some grown-ups were 'Key Workers' and so needed to continue working. Their children could still go to school, but it would all be different. One school in town would become a 'Hub School' and would take all the Key Workers' children from around the area and some of their teachers would go too.

Alexander and Lily were not at all happy. Just because their mum was a single mum and a nurse, they would have to go to this mini version of their school in the Hub School, whereas most of their friends got to stay at home. How could that be fair?

When they got home, they both protested to their mum.

"We don't want to go to the Hub School without our friends," Lily moaned, flicking her long brown ponytail and wrinkling the scattering of freckles over her nose.

"It will be weird to be in such a small class," added her brother. "And why should we have to travel all across town and go to a strange school?" Alexander complained.

"There really is no choice, I'm afraid," Mum said, sadly. "Since your dad died, we three are on our own here. And I *must* go to work; it's vital that we have as many nurses and all the other staff as possible or the hospital won't be able to cope with all these extra patients with this terrible virus!" she exclaimed.

"We know, Mum, but…" the children said together.

"No buts!" Mum stated firmly.

And that was that. What other option was there?

Chapter 2

The next day was Saturday and their mum's shift wasn't until the afternoon, so Lily and Alexander expected just a normal weekend morning.

But they were wrong.

"It's all sorted!" Mum announced proudly when the children appeared in the kitchen. "I will miss you both terribly, but I really do think that it's the best decision for you both. And it will make me less worried about you two catching the virus from me as I am still out and about."

"What is sorted, Mum?" asked Alexander.

"Tell us, Mum!" demanded Lily.

So their mother explained that she'd had a brainwave last evening after the children had gone to bed. One phone call later and it was all arranged.

And now Alexander and Lily found themselves on a train to a place they had never even heard of before. They would both have found it difficult to explain how they were feeling: it was a combination of worry, shock, sadness, anxiety, fear and excitement. Oh yes, definitely excitement amongst the more negative feelings!

They arrived eventually at a tiny station, got off the train and looked curiously at their surroundings. The station had no ticket office or waiting room. There was just a wooden bench on both platforms under white signs hung on little chains confirming that they were in Bixham. Best of all were the enormous flowerpots, full of beautiful daffodils and tulips. They wondered who looked after the plants in such a small station.

An elderly woman waved to them from the opposite platform. Carrying their cases, they crossed over the little footbridge and stood shyly in front of her.

She was dressed in the sort of soft, lightly checked brown trousers that their mum called 'slacks'. With these, she wore a pale blue jumper and a pearl necklace. She had old-fashioned leather sandals on her feet. Like their mother, this lady had pulled her hair into a bun, but her hair was white and the bun was on the top of her head. Their mother had chestnut brown hair, almost always tied in a bun at the nape of her neck. The old woman's green eyes were kind and her face suited the wrinkles around her smiling mouth.

"Welcome to Bixham!" the old woman exclaimed warmly. "Now, you must be Alexander, and you must be Lily," she continued, nodding to each child in turn.

They smiled rather awkwardly, not knowing quite what to say to this elderly lady.

"And of course you won't remember me, but I'm Minerva Nicholls."

"We met long ago when you were a baby, Lily, and Alexander was just the most adorable toddler!"

At these words, Alexander blushed scarlet to the roots of his ginger hair, temporarily hiding his freckles. The lady took no notice at all.

"You must call me Minnie, everyone does," she continued as she led the way out of the station through a gate set into a picket fence painted white.

The children were amazed at the only car parked neatly on the gravel road outside the station. It was red and shiny and about the oldest car they had ever seen outside a book or film. Minnie strapped their cases onto a wooden rack behind the back seat. Then she climbed into the driver's seat and invited them to join her, saying that whoever sat in the back today could sit in the front with her next time.

They were soon driving through the little village of Bixham, which turned out to be full of quaint cottages built from mellow sandy-coloured stones, many with thatched roofs.

In no time at all they were out into the countryside, passing fields with hedgerows full of wild primroses. They were surely only driving at about twenty miles an hour, but neither child had ever travelled in an open-top car before and it felt so much faster!

Already their mum and their home town felt a long, long way away.

Minnie turned into a driveway which curved through some very overgrown grass. She pulled up in front of a rather large building constructed from the same sandy yellow stones used in the village. Perhaps it had been grand once upon a time, with its red tiled roof, many chimneys and the stairs leading up to a massive green door with an enormous brass lion's head for a door knocker. There were more lions too, but these were even bigger and were standing guard on each side of the staircase.

But a closer look showed the children that it was no longer as grand as it probably had once been. The paint on the window frames was peeling, there was rust on the curved metal balustrades beside the stairs and one of the lion statues even had a chunk missing from the side of its mane where it had lost a piece of stone in some awful misfortune. This had almost certainly happened a long time ago as the area of the missing piece had weathered to a mottled green-grey to match the rest of the statue.

Suddenly the front door was flung open and an elderly man appeared, beaming widely.

"Welcome to Bixham Hall," the old couple cried in unison.

Chapter 3

Over a cup of tea and a slice of delicious home-made chocolate cake, their new hosts explained that they had been best friends with their grandparents many years ago.

"In fact, your mother used to call us Aunty Minnie and Uncle Arthur," Minnie told a surprised Alexander and Lily. "Of course we're not really family, but we were just as close when your mum was growing up."

"And as your mum didn't have any relations other than her parents – your grandparents – and we never had any children of our own, it was lovely for us all," Arthur continued.

"But why don't we know you both?" Alexander asked.

"Well, there were lots of changes all at once," Arthur said. "Your grandparents sadly died and then your poor dad died too. Then we inherited this old pile of stones from Minnie's uncle and decided to move here, so we lost touch with your mum."

"Not totally," Minnie corrected him. "After your dad died, your mum brought you both here to spend a little holiday away from town, but we did drift apart a bit after that. We still exchange Christmas cards, but we haven't actually all met up for a long while. Perhaps we remind your mum of all her unhappy times when she lost her parents and then your dad," concluded Minnie, sadly.

"But we're both delighted to help out in these strange times," Arthur said cheerfully and Minnie brightened.

"Yes," she said. "We were very glad to be able to invite you here. This virus is so bad, truly dreadful, but we will enjoy having you two about the place."

"You'll be safe in our home and you can explore the old grounds at the rear of the house to your hearts' content, even if they are quite ramshackle now!" exclaimed Arthur.

"We've never fully explored the garden ourselves, have we, Art?" Minnie said. "There are parts we've never even seen, so who knows what you might find!" she laughed.

Chapter 4

Arthur carried their cases and put them down at the top of the stairs. He told Lily and Alexander that they could choose a bedroom each, but only from those rooms in the East Wing.

"Up these stairs and turn right," he said. "You can explore all the rooms if you like; you'll soon find out why you can't have bedrooms in the West Wing."

The children had never been in such a big house before and they had great fun looking in all the rooms in the East Wing. Each room had various combinations of dark, old-fashioned furniture, but they both based their decisions on the colours of the wallpapers and the views from the windows.

Lily's room had pale blue striped wallpaper and a large bed with deep blue covers on it. Alexander's choice was the room next door, with dark green wallpaper and matching bed coverings. Both rooms had an excellent view looking over the garden behind the house. The children couldn't wait to go outside and explore, so they left the West Wing's discovery for another time.

Alexander and Lily found the old couple to be perfect hosts. They told the children that they were welcome to go wherever they wanted in the house and garden. There would be a cold supper later which could be eaten whenever they got hungry.

"We'll be working in the kitchen garden right outside the kitchen door over there," they said. "Come and find us when your tummies start rumbling!"

This total freedom was quite new to them and was strange at first. But as the days passed, they came to love it, along with loving Minnie and Arthur like new grandparents.

In fact, Arthur looked very much like their real grandfather in the photograph on their mantelpiece back home. Both men had snowy white hair and matching bushy moustaches. Neither child had been old enough to remember if their granddad had worn the same sort of clothes as Arthur, with his cardigans sporting leather patches over the elbows and the strange turn-ups and braces on his trousers.

The children spent the first couple of days exploring the grounds nearest the Hall. Most of it was quite overgrown, but became more and more like a jungle as they went further away from the house!

Their first discovery was the hen coop next to the kitchen garden at the back of the old house. Of course, both children knew that eggs are laid by chickens, but they had never seen actual hens before.

"Why are the chickens in that big cage?" they asked the elderly couple as they all tucked into their supper.

Smiling, Minnie explained that the cage part of the coop was to keep foxes out, rather than keep hens *in.*

"They have space in the coop to wander freely where they want and still be safe," she added.

"Our chickens roost in the wooden hen house at night," Arthur said. "Would you two like to help me collect up the eggs tomorrow morning?"

And so they did. The children enjoyed filling up the basket with eggs and they took on this job every morning after that. They soon learned to recognise individual hens and where they liked to lay their eggs. They fed the birds too, and quickly became very fond of them.

"These eggs taste better than the ones we usually have at home!" Lily told her brother, who nodded his agreement.

"And the fruit and vegetables from the kitchen garden here taste better too," he added.

One morning, they discovered the remains of an ancient ornamental fish pond and pulled some brambles away to reveal an old fountain shaped like a dolphin. It had obviously been a majestic feature once, but had been abandoned long ago.

On another occasion they found a wooden summerhouse. It was octagonal and was probably more than twice the size of their sitting room at home! Even though the wooden balustrade around it was quite dilapidated, the main floor of the summerhouse was still fine to sit on. The children enjoyed several picnics here in the sunshine.

The children found overgrown pathways and followed some of them as they tracked through the garden. Hedges and trees sprouted new growth in all directions but their strangest find of all was a long line of trees in the oddest shapes the children had ever seen. A stream ran across the middle of the line of weird trees but there was a pretty wooden bridge arching over it. The bridge had little wooden pagodas at each end and had once been painted red, although most of the paint had weathered away and only a few traces of it remained.

Over supper that day, Minnie told them that the peculiar trees had once been an avenue of topiary: yew trees clipped into enormous bird and animal shapes. These had taken professional gardeners many hours to create and keep clipped into perfect peacocks, foxes, teddy bears and so on. They were now going completely wild and had not resembled anything recognisable for a good many years.

"The knot garden is a bit like that," Arthur said. "It's made from box plants which are similar to yew but very much smaller. The box is planted in rows and circles to create a symmetrical pattern. Knot gardens go back a long way in history, but ours was planted in Victorian times. If you look carefully, you can still make out the original design."

As the children made their way upstairs to bed later, Alexander announced that they should look for the knot garden the very next day.

"Xander, I wonder what else there is here, that we haven't discovered yet!" Lily exclaimed.

Chapter 5

The next day dawned fine and bright, so the children did indeed set off to find the knot garden. They passed by the old pond and then the summerhouse; they'd never get to the far reaches of the grounds if they lingered here!

As they walked along the avenue of topiary, they had great fun trying to guess what these strange shapes had once been.

Lily said, "Isn't it funny how we are so busy here, with the hens and with all our exploring, Xander? I miss Mum, of course, but I have hardly thought about our friends at home at all!"

"You're right," said her brother. "I never knew that gardens and chickens would be such fun!"

They laughed, sauntering along happily together.

"We are so lucky to be here, Lils. Arthur and Minnie are very kind and this old place is wonderful. The TV news about the virus is terrible; I do hope that everyone back home is alright," he added.

Thoughtfully they continued through the garden and came to a small copse of trees.

"Are these fruit trees?" Lily asked.

But Alexander said, "I don't think so, Lils. These trees look too big to be fruit trees. I think this tall one here is an oak tree – look at the shape of the leaves. It looks just like the old oak tree in our school field, doesn't it?"

They continued on through the wood, ducking branches which grew at all odd angles and scrambling over a fallen tree lying forlornly on its side.

They passed into a clearing and then something very odd came into view.

"What is that, Xander?" Lily cried.

As if in silent agreement, they began to run together towards the strange sight.

They stopped when they were almost there. Standing before them was a sort of tiny castle. It had grey stone crenellated walls running right around it and a tower on one side. The tower seemed to be taller but its diameter looked about the same size as their house back home. This building looked older, though, much older.

"Let's go in!" Lily exclaimed excitedly, making for the rusty old wrought iron portcullis.

But her brother held her back.

"Wait, Lils,' he said. "We don't know if it's safe."

And so they circled round the tiny castle, looking intently as they went. The tower had very narrow openings but they were too high up to see into.

"For archers to attack enemies!" Alexander whispered, without knowing quite why he did so.

On the far side, the exterior wall had collapsed on one corner, so the children silently crept towards it and peered over. They faced a grassy area with a few piles of stones to one side where other small buildings had once stood.

"The green patch is for sword fighting and archery practice, Lils," Alexander muttered, recalling a school visit to a full-sized castle.

Lily nodded but couldn't speak as just then, the children got their first glimpse of the strangest sight they had ever seen!

Chapter 6

"Oh!" Lily gasped in surprise.

"Shh!" murmured her brother, giving her a gentle nudge with his elbow.

But it was too late!

The strangest creature they had ever clapped eyes upon lifted up its scaly head and turned around to see what had made the noise.

At once, both children ducked down out of sight behind the crumbling stones of the broken wall.

"Don't move!" Alexander whispered urgently. "Maybe it didn't see us.

Keep perfectly still!"

But as they waited, hardly daring to move, hardly daring to even *breathe,* the children could hear a snorting sort of breath and it was coming closer!

"It's coming! Let's run!" Lily suggested in the quietest voice she could manage in her panic.

"No, Lils." Alexander whispered. "Remember that nature film we saw with the grizzly bear? If we run, the beast will only chase us. Our best chance is to keep still and silent."

But that was so difficult. Both children were quaking with terror as the snorting, raspy breath from the other side of the wall got nearer and nearer.

There was a sudden noise as the creature climbed onto a fallen stone to see over the wall. Alexander grasped his sister's hand and both children held their breath.

What was the beast going to do?

A full minute passed and nothing happened. A minute is actually a very long time in circumstances such as these!

Slowly, Lily opened her eyes and was amazed at what she saw. A pair of eyes in a green, scaly face was looking down at them!

Lily squeezed her brother's hand and murmured softly, "I think it's OK, Xander. Look."

Cautiously, Alexander opened his eyes and found that Lily was right. The strange, green face looked somehow kind. The scaly animal was looking at them with as much curiosity as they were looking at *it*.

"Hello," Lily whispered. "You're friendly, aren't you?"

The creature jumped back in surprise, for it had never seen humans before and had never heard anyone speak!

"Poor thing," gasped Lily, "I didn't mean to frighten it! Did it fall off that stone?"

Both children stood up quickly and looked over the broken wall. They were just in time to see the strange beast fold its wings after fluttering safely down onto the ground.

"It's a dragon!" Alexander exclaimed excitedly.

"Shh!" whispered Lily. "We mustn't *scare* it!"

As they watched, the dragon puffed out a little plume of smoke. It regarded its visitors calmly with an interested expression. Its eyes were a soft grey and were surrounded by impressively long eyelashes. Its scaly body was mostly a deep green colour with a lighter green on its front. Its tummy was pale lime, as were its wings and claws.

"It's beautiful!" Alexander said in awe. "And I'm sure it's friendly."

Lily nodded her agreement with both of these statements and took a couple of steps towards the magnificent beast.

At once, the dragon backed up a few paces on its scaly feet.

"I think it's shy, Lils," Alexander said. "Let's not get any closer for now. Maybe it will get used to us and so let us get nearer next time."

The dragon gave them one last, long look then turned and waddled out of sight into the tower.

"Let's go back to the house now," suggested Alexander. "We can come back here and try again tomorrow."

So they made their way home, excitedly chatting about what they had found.

"They are real!" Alexander cried. "Who knew that dragons were real?"

"I never knew that dragons were so small," said his sister.

"Yes, the ones in stories are usually enormous," Alexander agreed. "And almost always ferocious," he added, thoughtfully.

"We wouldn't need Saint George for our dragon," Lily said. "But would *someone* come for it?" she continued. "Xander, I don't want anything nasty to happen to our dragon!"

Neither child noticed that they had somehow agreed to adopt it; it was no longer just any old dragon, but was now *their* dragon!

"Lils, let's keep it a secret for now," Alexander decided. "We won't tell anyone we've found a dragon until we know it's safe."

And so their plan was made: for now, their dragon would remain a secret!

Chapter 7

Both children were itching to visit the dragon again, but over breakfast the next morning, it began to drizzle. By the time they had fed the hens and collected up the eggs, the rain was pouring heavily.

"Let's go back in, Lils" Alexander said sadly. "Our dragon will have to wait another day!"

"Why don't we explore the house today instead," Lily suggested.

They started upstairs in the West Wing. Truth to tell, they had both been curious to look here, but the grounds had proven too exciting until now.

They soon understood exactly what Arthur had meant before. Room after room was in varying stages of decay. Wallpaper hung off many walls, the furniture was scratched and stained, and the curtains, rugs and bed coverings were mouldy. There was a damp, musty smell everywhere, but the worst thing of all was that the roof was leaking badly. There were buckets and bowls dotted all over the place collecting the rainwater which dripped in some places and trickled in others.

"Oh, here you are," Minnie gasped as the old couple rushed upstairs. "You have discovered the worst thing about Bixham Hall!"

"As you're here, perhaps you can help us empty out the buckets as they get fuller and fuller," Arthur suggested.

Of course the children gladly helped and they all had a very busy hour or so, carrying containers and tipping them out into the baths. Minnie and Arthur had developed a great system so they worked in pairs, one partner putting empty buckets in place as the other partner took away the full ones.

In this way they managed not to get the floors *too* wet. They took it in turns to carry the full containers but it was still hard work. Water is heavier than you might expect!

At last the rain eased and they all trooped downstairs for a cup of tea and a slice of cake.

"Nothing revives better than a cuppa and we all deserve some of Art's carrot cake after all that hard work!" exclaimed Minnie.

"Just wait until it rains heavily at night," Arthur sighed. "It's horrible having to get up at midnight to start work. And we have to keep it up until the rain stops!"

"It's even worse during the hours of darkness," Minnie added. "Because of all that rainwater we had to disconnect the electricity in the West Wing. We do have some oil lamps but the job is still much harder at night!"

"When Minnie inherited this old place, we sold our little house in town. We used most of that money fixing the bathrooms and putting in a new kitchen," Arthur explained. "There was only enough money left for half a new roof!"

They all laughed, but it clearly was a real problem. Minnie and Arthur were wonderful people and the children were sad that they couldn't afford to do all the repairs needed on the house. Bixham Hall needed so much doing to it.

Chapter 8

Lily and Alexander kept in regular contact with their mum by phone, but were both secretly glad that there was no internet connection at Bixham Hall. Once they'd done the homework set by their teachers on that strange last day in school, they were able to spend their unexpected free time however they wished: no internet so no online activities!

Luckily the weather kept fine for the next day, so they made their way back to the tiny castle as quickly as they could. When they came out of the copse, however, they slowed down and walked round to the wall's broken corner at the back. They didn't want to frighten the dragon by appearing too suddenly.

The children climbed over the enormous broken slabs of grey stone and looked around for the dragon. Disappointingly, it was nowhere to be seen.

"Hello dragon!" Alexander cooed in a soft voice. "Where are you?"

As if it understood these words, a green scaly head peeped out of the doorway of the little tower.

"There you are!" Lily called to it, copying her brother's soft tone of voice. "Can we come in your castle?" she asked.

Of course, the dragon didn't answer but it did come right out of the tower's doorway. The children were very pleased with this encouraging sign and took a couple of cautious steps towards it.

"Slowly," Alexander whispered to his sister. "Hopefully we can teach it that we mean it no harm."

Somehow, the dragon seemed to know that the children were friendly and didn't vanish back into its tower as it had before.

Encouraged, they waited for a few moments then took another couple of paces forward. The dragon appeared to accept them and even came a bit closer itself.

The three new friends looked at each other for a few minutes. The children smiled and cooed to it and held out their hands towards the dragon, but it came no nearer.

All of a sudden, it turned and fled back into the tower.

"Obviously, it's had enough for today. We'll come back tomorrow and maybe we can get even closer," Alexander said.

"I hope so," sighed Lily. "I'd love to stroke it," she added. "Did you see the row of spiky lime green scales on its back?"

"Yes. And they got smaller as they went down its tail – beautiful!" Alexander exclaimed, smiling.

"I noticed that the very tip of its tail was a triangular shape," Lily laughed.

Happily, the children walked back in the direction of the big, old house. They were delighted that their dragon had still been in the tiny castle and that the scaly animal was beginning to trust them.

They were near the line of topiary when Lily spotted a wall: a red brick wall. There was a brick arch in the middle and a gate made with interesting twists of metal.

No words were needed. In silent agreement the children tiptoed towards it and Alexander opened the gate.

But it was nowhere near as exciting as the dragon!

The red brick wall was actually built into a large square. Paths of a similar red brick criss-crossed the square both diagonally and through the middle. There was a statue of a man in the exact centre, bent forward as if he was running somewhere very fast. But the flowerbeds arranged in a symmetrical pattern were full of dead plants.

"Just boring old dead sticks!" Lily cried.

"Never mind," consoled her brother. "We've still got our secret dragon!"

"Xander, I wish we knew if it was a boy or girl dragon," Lily said. "It seems wrong to say 'it' instead of 'him' or 'her'."

"But how can we tell?" Alexander asked.

Neither child knew, so there was no answer to this question.

Chapter 9

Over breakfast the next day, Arthur noticed that both children seemed rather restless. Of course, he didn't know that they were longing to visit the dragon again.

"What are you two so excited about?" he asked.

Lily held her breath – how could they keep their dragon a secret?

But her brother quickly came up with an idea.

"We found a strange walled garden full of dead plants yesterday. We thought we'd go back there today and try to find out what it is," Alexander said.

Both children felt sorry about not telling the old couple what they were *really* excited about. Arthur and Minnie were so kind, but who knew how they would react if they heard about the tiny castle and its scaly creature? No, to be on the safe side, their dragon must remain a secret for now.

But the adults didn't notice the children's unease.

"It's not full of *dead* plants!" Minnie exclaimed, laughing. "It's a rose garden and it will be beautiful in a couple of months."

"Some plants are dormant in the winter, so they just *look* dead. But there will be leaves and buds and then wonderful flowers soon. In just a matter of weeks, the rose garden will be full of colourful flowers and wonderful scents. It will be very much alive and buzzing with insects," Arthur explained.

"What a coincidence that we're all talking about plants today," Minnie stated. "We thought that you would like to help us in our kitchen garden – what do you say?"

Of course, both children readily agreed to help, doing their best to look pleased. They were secretly disappointed that they couldn't immediately go back to their dragon again. Instead, they spent the next two days working in the ground's walled kitchen garden.

Minnie showed them how to sow seeds. Together they planted lots of vegetables that they'd heard of and some that they hadn't, such as kohlrabi.

"If you're here until these veg all grow, we can cook them up and you can find out what the more unusual ones taste like," Minnie promised.

In an ancient greenhouse, they planted trays of lettuce, rocket, herbs and tomatoes. Some of the glass panes were cracked, but Minnie told them that the greenhouse was still good enough for the salad and herb plants to grow well.

"As soon as they are big enough and we are certain that there will be no more frosts, we'll put all the seed trays outside anyway," she told them. "For a week or two, the seedlings will be out during the day and back inside the greenhouse at night. This is called 'hardening off'. Once the new plants are used to being outdoors, they can stay out."

With Arthur, they dug in seed potatoes, and then he showed them the fruit trees planted along the walls of the kitchen garden.

"These trees were already here when we got this place," Arthur said. "Their branches are spread out along the walls like this to save space but mostly to grow better with the warmth from the bricks in the sunshine," he added.

He taught the children how to cut off little stray branches and tie the new shoots onto the special wires criss-crossing the walls.

"We'll have apples, pears, blackberries and plums here," he said. "There are more fruit trees in the orchard – have you two found that yet?"

"No, not yet," Lily answered.

"Where is it?" Alexander asked.

"It's more fun to find it for yourselves!" chuckled the old man. "It's very overgrown like most of this ramshackle garden, but you'll know it when you find it. The trees are full of blossom at this time of year and the orchard is quite beautiful," he added.

Lily asked, "What trees are there in your orchard?"

"Apples, pears, quince, damsons and cherries," Arthur replied. "The trees have been here a long time; it takes a good many years for fruit trees to produce decent fruit. Gardening can be almost instant – you can get strawberries in a pot in a few months; however, damsons can take thirty years so gardeners have to learn patience!" he smiled. "Good things are well worth waiting for."

When the children sat down for a rest and a glass of home-made lemonade, they chatted about all the gardening they'd been doing. Their own garden was just a tiny square of lawn with some thin flowerbeds round the sides. Neither of them had ever been interested in helping their mum with it, but all that would change when they got home!

Chapter 10

As most of the planting in the kitchen garden had now been done, the children were free again to do what they wanted. So the following morning found them racing eagerly back to the tiny castle. They hadn't been able to visit for two whole days. Would their dragon still be there?

Knowing how shy their dragon was, they crept quietly round to the crumbling wall of the little castle. As they gazed around for their green dragon, both children gasped in delight at what they saw.

Yes, their dragon was still there. Better still, there were now *two* dragons!

"Look!" Lily whispered excitedly.

"There's a baby!" Alexander murmured joyfully.

At last the children had the answer to their previous question: the green dragon was obviously female!

"Xander, isn't it cute?" exclaimed Lily, clambering right over slabs of grey stone.

"Steady, Lils," Alexander cautioned gently, following his sister right into the castle grounds.

At once the mother dragon folded a lime green wing protectively around her baby. The youngster looked so adorable as it peeped out curiously at the children.

They were both encouraged that the mother didn't rush her baby back into the tower.

Slowly, very slowly, they approached. The children took just a couple of cautious steps towards the dragons and then paused. In this way, they hoped not to scare the scaly creatures.

"So cute!" Lily repeated softly, holding out her hand to the baby.

The mother dragon seemed to recognise the children and didn't appear to be frightened, but it was actually her baby who accepted that these newcomers were friends.

All of a sudden, the tiny dragon ran forward to Lily and rubbed its head on her legs, just like a cat would!

Overjoyed, Lily stroked the little animal and it lifted up its head for more petting of its neck.

Alexander tiptoed nearer until he, too, could stroke the little dragon.

"Aren't the baby's scales soft?" Lily said in wonder. "Not at all like I expected."

"Yes, even the pointy scales on the ridge of its back are silky. Perhaps they get pricklier as the dragon grows," suggested Alexander.

"Your baby is so beautiful!" Lily cooed and perhaps the mother understood as she waddled a little closer.

And the baby dragon was indeed beautiful. It had a pale mauve front but most of its body was a delightful deep purple which gleamed in the sunlight. Its tummy, wings, claws, pointy ridge scales and the triangular tip of its tail were of such a light lilac that they seemed almost white.

"You are absolutely wonderful," Alexander said tenderly, tickling the baby under its little chin.

Suddenly, the baby hiccupped and puffed a little plume of white smoke out of its purple nostrils. Both children giggled in delight and the tiny dragon wiggled its little wings as it seemed to chuckle too.

Then the little dragon yawned widely, revealing one solitary tooth. As it scuttled back to its mother, she unfolded one lime green wing to usher it back into the tower.

"Time for its nap!" Alexander exclaimed. "And time for us to head for home. Goodbye, dragons."

"Goodbye dragons," Lily echoed. "See you tomorrow!"

After strolling through the copse of trees, the children turned right instead of their usual left towards the house. What would they find if they went this way?

First there was an old wooden fence with a stile set in the middle to climb over it. Then they trekked across a meadow which had had sheep in it many years before but was now so overgrown that it was difficult to walk through.

Next the children came to a little brook which trickled across the end of the meadow. It then snaked out of the grounds of Bixham Hall and off into the distance in a westerly direction.

"This must run east into the stream in the middle of the topiary avenue," Lily said. "But there's no bridge here."

Luckily, there were some stepping stones in the water and both children chuckled as they jumped from stone to stone. The water was shallow and rather cold but neither child minded when it splashed them.

And then they saw clouds of blossom ahead of them.

"The orchard!" they yelled in unison, running towards it.

"Art was quite right," Alexander said. "It is beautiful!"

And indeed it was. The orchard was full of trees, all smothered in magnificent blossom. The children couldn't identify any of the trees, but they relished their many colours. The blossom ranged from creamy whites, to the palest pinks and mauves, right through to deep pinks and purples.

"We'll definitely come back here again," Lily declared. "And then we can pick some of the fruits and find out which trees are which."

"I wonder how long this lockdown will last?" Alexander said. "Will we still be here when the fruits are ripe enough to pick?"

But there was no way to answer this question.

Chapter 11

The children chatted about their dragons all the way back to the old house. Now that they knew for certain that the green dragon was female, they decided to consider the baby to be a boy.

"It doesn't really matter if the little one is a girl anyway," Alexander said. "It just seems nicer somehow to have a girl and a boy dragon."

His sister agreed, but what they couldn't decide upon was what to call them. None of their suggestions seemed right. What names would be best for the dragons?

Minnie suddenly appeared from the kitchen garden. Alexander nudged Lily to be quiet, but it was too late!

"Good names for dragons?" Minnie asked.

"Er, yes," Alexander said quickly. "We're, um, thinking about writing a story with dragons…" He tailed off limply, hating that he was trying to deceive Minnie. But he didn't want to tell her about their scaly new friends until he was sure that it was safe. There are simply too many tales of people slaying dragons!

"Well, I think that Zelda would be a good name for a dragon," Minnie suggested, "if it's a girl dragon."

"Perfect!" Lily cried and ran to hug Minnie.

If Minnie was surprised, she didn't show it. Minnie seemed to take everything in her stride!

That evening, both children were sitting on the bed in Alexander's room, discussing their dragons, of course.

"I think that Art and Minnie are so lovely. We *can* trust them with our dragons!" declared Lily.

Alexander believed that she was right, but he wanted to check somehow. Both children pondered this problem until he suddenly had a good idea.

"Lils, let's ask Minnie and Arthur what they would do if a fox got in the hen coop and ate a chicken. If they say that they would let the fox go free, we might be able to trust them with our dragons. What do you think?"

Lily readily agreed and they resolved to put their plan into practice the next day.

A perfect opportunity presented itself after breakfast. The children had already fed the hens and collected up the eggs when Arthur asked them to help him and Minnie to water all the fruits and vegetables in the kitchen garden.

As they filled up the watering cans from the water butt, Arthur explained how the rainwater ran down the roof, went down the drainpipes and was collected by the water barrel at the bottom.

"We get most water here from the roof over the East Wing," he laughed. "Too much rain drips into the inside of the West Wing!"

"Arthur, Minnie," Alexander began cautiously, "what would you do to a fox if you found it in the hen house?"

"We wouldn't do anything to it!" Arthur declared. "The fox would only be following its natural instinct to hunt."

Minnie nodded and added, "We wouldn't be *happy* if any of our hens were killed by a fox, of course we wouldn't. But foxes are beautiful animals and they get hungry too!"

Lily was just about to tell the kind, old couple about their dragons, when Minnie invited the children into the greenhouse to look at the seed trays they had planted up together.

"Some of the seeds are starting to sprout," she said. "It's so exciting!"

Indeed it was exciting. Some tiny leaves were already pushing their way up through the soil.

"Are the seedlings ready to go outside now?" Lily asked.

"No, not yet," Minnie replied. "When they are all a bit bigger, we will start to harden them off. Do you remember what that means?"

The children nodded as Arthur continued, "When the seedlings are stronger we will replant them into bigger pots."

"Some will be planted directly in one of the vegetable beds," said Minnie.

"We never realised that there's so much to do with plants," Alexander said. "But we've found that we *love* gardening. We hope to do some planting of our own when we get home, don't we Lils?"

"Yes. We never knew that gardening was such fun!" Lily exclaimed, making the adults laugh.

"We're not at school but we are learning so much!" Alexander said.

"Thanks so much for having us to stay here; we love it!" Lily stated.

"And we love having you two here!" Arthur said and his wife nodded and smiled.

The four of them fell naturally into a group hug and then the children set off to explore again.

Chapter 12

Peering over the broken wall of the tiny castle, the children were delighted to see their dragons again. There they were, on the green in front of them, and a lesson seemed to be in progress.

Quietly, the children climbed onto one of the stone slabs lying on its side. They settled down to watch the dragon school!

Zelda – yes, she *did* suit this name – puffed out a plume of smoke through her green nostrils. The baby blew and blew, but only succeeded in blowing snorty raspberries!

Both children giggled even though they admired the youngster's resilience. Time and again his mother showed him how to puff smoke; time and again he tried and failed.

At last, he succeeded in puffing out a little smoke and the children clapped their hands. Luckily, neither dragon was frightened, and somehow they even seemed to be pleased with this encouragement.

Dragon school progressed into the next lesson. Zelda produced a raspy roar and a flame of fire shot out of her mouth. Alexander, Lily and the baby were all impressed.

Yet again, the baby tried and tried. He managed to make a little raspy roar of his own, but no flame appeared.

Time and again Zelda roared and produced flames; time and again her baby managed a little roar but no fire at all.

However, the baby was made of stern stuff and he did not give up. He tried and tried, eventually producing his little raspy roar and a shower of orange and yellow sparks.

Again, the children clapped and the dragons looked as if they were smiling in pleasure.

The baby came over to the children and they stroked him lovingly. Zelda waddled over too and Alexander reached out a hand to her. He was overjoyed when she came a bit closer and he was able to stroke her as well.

As Lily continued to pet the youngster, he yawned widely.

"Breathing fire is obviously tiring!" she said, giggling.

Zelda clearly thought so too, as with a little waggle of her wings to say farewell, she ushered her baby into the tower for a well-deserved rest.

Chapter 13

Ambling away, they headed for the old summerhouse where they sat down and enjoyed the picnic lunch Arthur had prepared for them.

"How did Zelda feel?" Lily asked curiously. "I hope that I can stroke her next time."

"Her scales are definitely harder than the baby's and the ridge ones are a bit prickly. The other scales are still quite soft, though. Not like I imagined," he considered.

"The baby is so good, isn't he, Xander?" Lily said. "He just never gives up. His little sparks were so pretty. And he still only has one tooth – I saw it when he yawned," she smiled.

"I've got it!" Alexander cried suddenly. "Let's call him 'Sparky'."

"Perfect!" his sister agreed.

But then her expression grew serious. "But what about our other problem? Shall we share our secret dragons with Art and Minnie or not?"

"I've been thinking about that too, Lils," said Alexander. "Arthur and Minnie both said that they wouldn't hurt a fox, even if it killed one of their chickens. I'm sure that we could trust *them* with our dragons. But what about *other* adults? I'm worried that Art and Minnie would have to report the dragons. There might be a law about it. I just don't know," he concluded sadly.

"We've never met any other dragons or even seen them on the telly."

"Are they against the law? You know what grown-ups are like about following the rules. I don't want our wonderful dragons to be in danger!" Lily declared.

"Let's think some more about it," Alexander suggested.

"I do feel bad that we're not being honest. But if we tell them about our dragons we can't un-tell them if it all goes wrong," Lily shook her head sorrowfully.

"Let's not say anything for now and we'll come to a decision after we've thought some more about it," Alexander said and Lily agreed.

When they got back to the house later, the children found Arthur and Minnie in the hallway.

"We're expecting a grocery delivery any minute now," Minnie said.

"If you hear the door knocker, do *not* open the door!"

"But you have all your own food already," Lily cried in surprise.

"Oh yes, we have our own eggs and there are plenty of fruit, vegetables, salads and herbs. Our freezer is full and our cupboards are almost bursting with jams, pickles and preserves. But we still need to buy some things from the shops, don't we, Art?"

"Oh yes," he replied. "No-one has invented a toilet roll tree yet!"

Everyone was still laughing when there came a knock on the door.

"Keep right back," Minnie instructed.

Arthur waited a minute or two before opening the front door. On the top step, next to the rusty balustrade, were two bulging shopping bags. At the bottom of the steps, right away from the door, stood a bearded young man with fair hair flopping over his face. He was wearing scruffy jeans, trainers and a black t-shirt emblazoned with the name and logo of his favourite pop group. He waved to Arthur and Minnie.

"Hello," he called. "How are you?"

"We're fine, thanks Donnie. Are you and your family all doing well in these strange times?"

"Everyone is very well, thanks Art. The lockdown and the social distancing are difficult, but they are keeping us all safe, thank goodness. Let me know what else you need and I'll be back in a fortnight's time. Stay safe!" he said.

And with a farewell wave, he was gone.

"We are so lucky that Bixham is such a friendly village. Volunteers like Donnie are doing a marvellous service for the whole community, bless them!" Minnie exclaimed as Art carried in the shopping and began sorting items.

"Minnie," Lily began cautiously, "are there any unusual animals in this area?"

Alexander shot her a worried frown, but Minnie didn't seem to notice anything unusual about the question.

"No, I don't think so," she replied. "A few years ago there was talk of a panther on the moors twenty miles away from Bixham, but no-one could prove that it was really there. Probably just someone's imagination."

"Or somebody's idea of a joke," Arthur said. "But we do have lots of wildlife in this neighbourhood: foxes, badgers, squirrels, frogs and toads, owls and loads more. We're very lucky around here," he declared.

"But no panthers!" Minnie exclaimed.

Chapter 14

Arriving at the tiny castle the very next morning, the children were surprised to see Zelda sitting on top of the crenellated wall which encircled the little fortress. They called a soft-voiced hello so as not to startle her. She glanced at them and puffed a grey plume of smoke as if in reply.

The children climbed onto a stone slab at the broken corner of the wall and were even more surprised to find Sparky also on top of two stones in the crumbling section. What was going on?

Intrigued, they watched as Zelda unfolded her wings and gently fluttered them. The baby copied his mother, flapping his wings enthusiastically.

Then Zelda stretched out her wings and glided down onto the grass. Sparky tried to drift down as well, but he just couldn't do it. Again and again he stretched out his little wings without success.

Lily murmured, "Dragon school for Sparky again."

"I don't think his wings are strong enough yet," Alexander whispered back.

Zelda joined her baby on his stones and picked him up by carefully putting her mouth around the ridge scales on the back of his neck. Together they extended their wings and together they floated down onto the grass with Zelda still holding her baby.

Lily muttered excitedly, "She's teaching Sparky to fly!"

Entranced, the children looked on as the dragons repeated these movements. Sometimes, the mother held on to Sparky and glided with him held in her mouth; sometimes Zelda flew up higher and demonstrated perfect wing actions to float down to the ground. Although he watched his mother carefully and tried to copy her many times, poor Sparky never succeeded.

At last, after a joint effort, the tiny purple dragon collapsed onto the grass where he lay, panting.

Immediately, Zelda picked him up and flew with her baby back to the little tower. She turned in the doorway and glanced at the children as if to say farewell, then the two scaly creatures vanished inside.

"Poor little Sparky. It must be hard work learning to fly!" Lily exclaimed.

"Next time I struggle with something, Lils, I'm going to remember our baby dragon. Robert the Bruce was inspired by a spider and we've learned resilience from little Sparky!" Alexander announced.

"It's funny, isn't it? We're not at school but being in Bixham is teaching us so much," replied his sister, smiling.

When the children got back to the house, Arthur asked them to join him in the kitchen. He had sorted out some food items from the back of the cupboards and arranged them on the worktop.

"Look here," he said. "I thought it would be a good idea for us to use some ingredients which we've had in our cupboards for a while. Even with Donnie's kind deliveries, we're not buying all of our usual shopping. "

At once they agreed to help. Arthur gave each child a cook book, telling them to look at the foods he'd found and then search for recipes which they would like to try using these ingredients.

So Alexander and Lily helped Arthur to plan their meals for the next couple of days. They had both done a bit of cooking before at home and at school, but had never read through cook books or considered ingredients in this way before.

Minnie came in from the kitchen garden and showed the children how to prepare baking tins and set the oven to the correct temperature.

"Now comes the really fun part!" Arthur said.

And the children found that he was right. They both enjoyed helping the old couple to weigh and mix, learning special food terms like cream together, fold in and knead. Minnie explained the differences between teaspoons, dessert spoons and tablespoons. Neither child had realised before how complicated cookery was!

"Now for the hard part," said Arthur.

The children looked puzzled.

"We must wait until the foods are cooked and we'll get hungry with all the wonderful baking smells!" Minnie stated.

All four of them enjoyed a feast that evening, topped off with Arthur's caramel apple pie which he served with vanilla ice cream.

"We'll definitely do some cooking when we get home," Alexander said. "Mum would love all this, wouldn't she, Lils?"

"Yes! Everything home-made tastes so much better!" Lily exclaimed in wonder.

And they all laughed happily together.

Chapter 15

"We've been so lucky with the weather," stated Lily the next morning as they fed the chickens and collected eggs. "Mum is so right when she says we must count our blessings."

Alexander nodded his agreement, then called to the hens:

"Have a lovely day in the sunshine, ladies, and thanks for our eggs. We had a tasty breakfast!" He chuckled, making his sister giggle too.

Alexander looked thoughtful as they walked through the grounds to the tiny castle.

"You know, Lils, the news on the telly is terrible about all those poor people ill or dying with this virus. But one really positive thing for us is that we've spent so much time together and had such fun. I miss Mum and all my friends, but it's good that we've got much closer, isn't it?" Alexander considered.

Lily nodded, took his hand and squeezed it. It seemed perfectly natural now to hold hands, something which they never did at home, not since they were tiny.

Suddenly, normality returned. Dropping hands, they ran towards the little castle and round to the wall's crumbling corner.

But the dragons were nowhere to be seen!

"Where are they?" Lily cried. "I hope they've not gone!"

"Let's go right in and look for them," suggested Alexander. "Quietly, we don't want to scare our dragons if we find them," he warned.

It was the very first time that the children had been right inside and it felt rather strange. They explored every part of the little fortress, finding things which they had never seen before. There were several recesses in the wall which encircled it that could not be seen from outside the castle. These recesses were rather black and the children realised that they had once been fireplaces.

Towards the dragons' tower, some of the remains of rooms were several layers higher than those they had seen near the broken corner of the outside wall. There were gaps in some walls which Alexander thought could be doorways although the wooden doors had rotted away many years before.

But their best find was a small metal object which Lily spotted as it glinted in the sunlight. It was flat and almost circular, though the edges were a bit battered now. Excitedly the children thought that it was a coin and examined both sides carefully, hoping to see some details and perhaps even the head or name of an old king or queen. Sadly any distinguishing marks had vanished long ago, after many seasons on the ground. Nonetheless, they were delighted with this find and Alexander put it safely away in the very bottom of the pocket in his jeans.

Eventually, there was only one place left to search and so they entered the dragons' little tower. This was the most complete part of the castle and the children found themselves in a little room which also had an old fireplace in it. There were stone steps in one corner leading upwards in a spiral.

"Hello dragons," Lily cooed softly, but the scaly creatures were not at home.

Alexander said, "They've definitely been here only a short time ago. Come over here, Lils."

As the children held out their hands in front of the fireplace, they could still feel some warmth from the embers of fire which must have been blazing before the dragons left.

"Look in the ashes here," Lily said. "Pieces of egg shell."

Jubilant, they realised what this meant. Little Sparky had been in the egg and emerged here as a baby dragon!

"Cute!" Lily smiled and her brother nodded.

"OK. Let's go up these stairs," Alexander said.

They did so and it was immediately obvious that Zelda would be too big to climb the stairs even though she was much smaller than the fierce dragons found in stories. Many of the steps were worn where many human feet had trod over the years, but with care they were still safe to use.

"Being on the inside has protected them from the weather," Lily whispered.

The children passed several flat steps which were much larger than the others. These corresponded with the slits for archers which they had noticed when they first visited the fortress, although that seemed like quite a while ago. Lily was disappointed that she wasn't tall enough to see through them, but this feeling disappeared when they reached the top and stepped out into the sunlight. Both children blinked as the light was so bright after the gloomy stairwell; then they were able to admire the fantastic view.

Of course, the tower was not as tall as a tower in a full-sized castle, but the view was still spectacular. From here, the children could see the grounds of Bixham Hall laid out before them. They marvelled at the size of the garden, as they had when they'd first arrived. Now that they had visited almost all parts, they were able to distinguish the meadow, the stream and even the old summerhouse. But there was a large, flat area right over to the east which they had never seen before. As it shimmered in the sunlight, the children resolved to visit it at their first opportunity.

In the distance they could see some of the countryside around Bixham Hall, but they couldn't make out the train station. Even the back of the Hall was too distant to be clear from this viewpoint, but they hardly noticed that.

For at that very moment, they both heard something strange and it seemed to be coming closer. What was it?

The children turned round and saw something wonderful, almost magical. It was Zelda and the odd sound was the swishing noise her wings made as she flew towards them. She carried her baby in her mouth as she had before. Little Sparky was fluttering his wings too, obviously practising although he couldn't fly on his own yet.

There was no mistaking the joy of both scaly creatures as Zelda swooped around the tower. Expertly, she landed right next to the children and placed Sparky gently on the stone viewing platform. The tiny dragon ran to Alexander and nestled against his legs as the boy stroked him. Lily reached out to Zelda and was delighted when the green dragon allowed her to stroke her scales as well.

Then Sparky amazed the children by hopping up to the castellated edge of the tower, using his little wings to help lift himself up. As Zelda looked on approvingly, he spread his wings fully and jumped right over the edge. Lily gasped and her brother held his breath, but they need not have worried as the purple dragon glided confidently down to the grass below.

"Well done, Sparky!" Lily called.

"And well done to you as well," Alexander said to Zelda. "You have taught him well and he is building up the strength in his wings."

Perhaps she understood him, for she puffed out a plume of smoke then flew down to join her youngster.

The children followed down the steps but went very slowly and carefully as the spiral stairs seemed somehow steeper than on the way up. Leaving the tower, they found the dragons resting in a sunny spot on the grass. They sat with their scaly friends for a few minutes, then Sparky yawned and Zelda took him into the tower for a nap. The children were near enough to see them both curl up together in front of the old fireplace.

"Goodbye," Alexander said.

"See you tomorrow," his sister added as they scrambled over the broken stones and headed out of the castle.

Chapter 16

"Lils, let's go east now," Alexander suggested. "We can try to find that big shimmery place which we saw from the top of the tower."

"What do you think it is?" Lily asked, but her brother was not sure.

So they wandered through the copse and turned left to walk east. They did not have to go far before the mystery was solved. A huge expanse of water came into view.

"Another pond!" Lily exclaimed, but her brother shook his head.

"No, I think it's much too big to be a pond, Lils," he said. "This is a lake and it's quite a large lake!"

"Look over there, Xander," his sister cried, pointing. "The stream leads to this lake."

The children did not know if the lake was natural or man-made, but its shape looked natural. There were trees and a path running right around it and they needed no encouragement to set off on the walkway which had been created many years ago. Here and there old stone benches made from the same grey stones as the tiny castle. The seats were quite weathered and the ones in the shadows from the nearby trees were covered in moss. In between the benches, set back a little from the path, were interesting statues. The children enjoyed finding these and counted twelve in total.

They chose a nice sunny bench to sit on and gazed over the water. There were lots of birds, including ducks, coots and moorhens which they recognised from the river on the far side of their home town. There were also many other birds which they couldn't name, including one standing near the water's edge which was very much bigger than all the others. It had very long, skinny legs, a long body and a long neck. It was mostly grey with white underneath, had an enormous beak and long feathers on the top of its head which angled backwards and matched the long feathers at its throat.

"What on Earth is that?" asked Alexander, pointing to the strange bird.

"It's massive!" Lily gasped and both children fell into a fit of giggles.

"We'll ask Art and Minnie later," said Alexander when their giggles had subsided.

"Xander, there's fish too," Lily cried and both children saw the ripples in the water as the fish swam by.

"I wonder what sort of fish they are," Alexander said. "There's an awful lot of things we don't know, isn't there, Lils?" he added sadly.

For the second time that day, Lily took his hand and squeezed it.

Then she stood up and pointed to another path snaking southwards away from the lake.

"Let's see where that goes," she suggested and her brother stood up as well.

They followed the path until a red brick wall came into sight.

"We must be on the other side of the rose garden," Alexander declared, trotting forward and opening a metal gate which was the identical twin of the gate they had opened before at the other end of the walled garden.

But this visit was not as disappointing as their first. The plants were still rather bare at first glance, but a closer inspection revealed little leaves beginning to develop. Better still, some of the rose bushes even had tiny buds on them.

"Art and Minnie were right," Lily stated. "New life is already sprouting here."

"I wonder if we'll get to see the roses in full bloom," Alexander said.

But there was no way to answer this question, so neither child fretted about it. Instead, they walked out through the gate they had used before, but turned left this time instead of right back to the house.

Following a cobbled pathway through some quite long grass, the children were surprised to find another little wall. This one was not red, but was a mellow sandy yellow colour like the Hall and the cottages in the village.

The children went through the wall's yellow brick archway and looked curiously around.

Suddenly, they cried in unison: "The knot garden!"

"I'd almost forgotten all about it," Alexander admitted.

Lily nodded and added, "It seems like ages ago that we all talked about it. So much has happened since then!"

Although the little box plants were indeed overgrown, as Arthur had said, it was still possible to see the patterns once created by the Hall's gardeners. The box plants still displayed their original geometric lines and circles, all arranged in a symmetrical pattern leading to a small circle at the exact centre. Inside this circle was a statue of a boy playing panpipes.

"I think he is called Pan," Alexander told his sister, but he couldn't remember who Pan was.

"We'll ask Minnie and Arthur," Lily said. "They are so clever; they seem to know everything!"

Chapter 17

Supper later was walnut and mushroom Wellington, another of their bakes from the previous day. None of them had tried it before, but Alexander had found the recipe in his cookbook and chosen it to use up a packet of walnuts which Arthur had found at the back of the cupboards. Everyone thought it was delicious, and Arthur said that he would definitely make another Wellington in the future.

Pleased with this success, Alexander asked the elderly couple about the large bird that they had seen at the lake.

"It sounds like a heron," Minnie said. "We can look it up in my bird spotters' guide."

She left the kitchen and returned a few minutes later with a little book and a pair of binoculars.

"I thought that you two might like these," she said, giving the book to Alexander and the binoculars to Lily.

While Arthur showed Lily how to use the binoculars, her brother looked in the index at the back of the little book. He found 'heron' and turned to the indicated page.

"This is it!" he exclaimed. "Our big bird was a heron!"

Lily looked at the picture in the spotter's guide and agreed with him.

"Keep the book and the binoculars," Minnie told the children. "We've had great fun with them in the past and I think that it should be your turn now."

"Thank you," the children cried together, both pleased with the unexpected gifts.

Arthur and Minnie were so generous in every way, including their time, advice and hospitality. Both children felt very lucky to be staying at the Hall with them.

Arthur said, "The pictures in the guide are excellent, so it's easy to identify birds that you see when you are out exploring. The book is small enough to put in your pocket and then it's handy to refer to when you are out and about."

At the mention of the word 'pocket', Alexander suddenly remembered the coin which they had found in the tiny castle.

"I had forgotten all about this!" he exclaimed, taking out the coin and holding it up for everyone to see.

"We found it in the tiny castle when we were looking for our dragons," Lily said, without thinking first about what she was saying.

There was a stunned silence for a moment or two, which seemed like an age to the children. Lily bit her lip while Alexander held his breath.

Were the dragons in danger now that their secret was out?

The children need not have feared, however. Once again, the kind old couple were able to take everything in their stride.

"Well," Minnie began, "let's start by having a look at what you've found."

Alexander passed her the coin and she looked curiously at both sides then passed it to her husband.

"It's very weathered," Arthur said, after a thorough examination.

"It's a pity because we can't make out any of the details it may have once had. There's no telling how old it is or where it came from."

He gave the coin back to Alexander, telling him to keep it for good luck. Neither child knew it then, but in the future they would take turns with the coin and would both believe that it did indeed bring them good luck!

"Now, let's put the kettle on and perhaps you two could tell us about your discoveries; most exciting and most mysterious!" Minnie declared.

Lily glanced at her brother, wondering if he was cross with her for blurting out their secret. However, he smiled, took her hand and squeezed it comfortingly.

Feeling reassured, Lily began to tell their elderly friends all about the exploring that she and Alexander had undertaken. She talked about the fish pond, the summerhouse, the orchard and the overgrown meadow.

"You already know about us finding the rose garden and the avenue of topiary trees," Lily continued.

The old couple nodded and told the children that they also knew about all of these areas in their grounds.

Lily paused and looked to Alexander to continue.

"We also found a brook with stepping stones across it and a stile over a wooden fence," he said.

"The fence looked like it was made from enormous lollipop sticks!" Lily added, making Minnie and Arthur laugh.

"We've never visited the far reaches of the grounds, have we Minnie?" Arthur said. "But that sounds like a fenced meadow where they used to keep sheep."

"You are right," she replied. "We always concentrate our efforts on the parts nearer the house, especially the hen coop and the kitchen garden. They are enough for our old bones!" she smiled.

"Well, on the other side of the wooden fence is a grey stone…" Alexander began.

Lily interrupted excitedly, "But we usually get there by going along the topiary avenue, over the little bridge and through a copse of trees."

"Get where*?*" Minnie asked mildly.

In their eagerness to tell them all about the tiny castle and their dragons, the children cried in unison: "The little castle where our dragons live!"

Their words seemed to hang in the air for a long moment before settling upon everyone in the room.

"A castle? We didn't know about that," Arthur said.

"Dragons?" asked Minnie. "We've certainly never found any dragons!"

Chapter 18

So the children explained about the tiny castle, the crumbling corner where they could get in, the tower and the two scaly creatures.

Arthur and Minnie surprised the children. They were neither disbelieving nor cross that the dragons had been a secret. Both youngsters had known all along that the elderly couple were friendly and kind, but the question about the safety from *other* adults still remained.

It was Alexander who voiced their fears when he said, "Is there a law against dragons? Do we have to report them? Will the authorities come and capture them or even slay them?"

But reassurance from the grown-ups came swiftly.

"No, there is nothing like that. For sure there are no laws against dragons," Arthur declared.

"It's simply that there are so few dragons about. Most people think of them only as characters in stories," Minnie added.

"But they *are* real!" exclaimed Lily.

"Quite so," Arthur stated solemnly. "And I'm sure that I can speak for both of us when I say that we are looking forward to seeing them tomorrow," he concluded and Minnie nodded, smiling.

The next day was another fine, sunny spring day. After breakfast and seeing to the hens and watering in the kitchen garden, the four humans set off to visit the dragons. As they walked along, the children told the older couple all about their scaly friends. Minnie and Arthur were most interested in every detail and it seemed like no time at all until the little fortress came into view.

"Wow, just look at that!" exclaimed Minnie. "All these years since I inherited Bixham Hall and we never even guessed that this was here!"

Both grown-ups looked to the children to lead them to the dragons.

"We need to go quietly so as not to scare them," Lily advised in a soft voice.

They all crept around the castle and peeped in over the crumbling corner. The dragons were not there!

Alexander and Lily climbed over the broken slabs of grey stone and entered the green area where knights may once have practised their archery and sword skills. Despite their advanced ages, both Arthur and Minnie followed suit. The four of them sat upon a stone slab each and waited expectantly. Had the dragons gone for good?

But no; soon there came the noise of beating wings and the dragons flew over the castle. Maybe they had already seen their visitors, for they landed close to where they were sitting.

Minnie and Arthur found it quite difficult not to gasp or cry out in awe, as the dragons folded their wings and looked curiously at *them.*

Just as before, it was the baby who made the first move. Perhaps he understood that the two newcomers were friendly as they sat with the children. Or perhaps he was simply able to recognise that these adults were good people. Whatever his reasoning, he scuttled over to Minnie and nuzzled around her legs in the same manner as a cat.

"You are gorgeous," she laughed as she stroked little Sparky.

Zelda puffed out a little plume of smoke by way of greeting the visitors.

Arthur was enchanted and held out his hand to her, but she was too shy to come any nearer. But her baby toddled over to him for a stroke, and then hopped right onto Alexander's knee with a quick flutter of his wings. Both children petted him while Zelda watched approvingly.

Soon the baby was yawning and Lily was delighted to see that he now had two spiky teeth.

Sparky scooted over to join his mother and together they waddled towards the doorway of the little tower. Before vanishing inside, Zelda turned and waggled her wings as if in farewell, then they were gone.

Chapter 19

Everyone chatted cheerfully as they strolled back home.

"Wonderful. What majestic creatures!" cried Minnie.

"And to think that we've been living here for years and never knew what magical animals lived in the grounds of Bixham Hall!" Arthur exclaimed.

Both children were overjoyed that their elderly friends had accepted their dragons. They knew now for sure that they were safe.

Minnie said, "We'll visit the dragons again tomorrow. Art, don't you think that Sparky is doing so well with his flying; like baby birds who soon get the hang of it."

"Zelda is obviously a good teacher and his little wings looked quite strong. Absolute magic!" he concluded and everyone agreed happily.

With great eagerness, the humans returned to the tiny castle on the very next morning. There was no sign of the scaly animals so they entered and sat, waiting once more.

They waited and waited, but still no dragons appeared.

The children became quite anxious. Where were the dragons?

"Patience," Arthur cautioned. "Wildlife doesn't run on timetables, like trains!"

Everybody tried to smile at his joke, but it needed a big effort.

Had something awful happened to the dragons?

Still they waited, yet the dragons did not arrive.

"Let's go in their tower and look for clues," suggested Alexander.

Lily readily agreed and skipped ahead of the others.

"No sign of them," she shouted sadly.

But when Alexander joined her with the two adults in tow, he *did* spot something unusual.

"Look!" he yelled excitedly, pointing to the fireplace.

And so they all gathered round and gazed into the fireplace together. Something was gleaming among the cold embers of the fire. What was it?

The children reached in and found not one, but *two* objects which shone in the shaft of sunlight from the doorway.

Each child held something cold and solid in their hands. Everyone was stunned into silence for a few seconds.

"It's beautiful," Lily whispered, as she held out her hand for them all to see.

There, in the palm of her hand, was an emerald, green and sparkling and as big as a hen's egg.

"Look at mine!" said Alexander.

He had a little purple gemstone in his hand. It was smaller than Lily's, but still it glittered in the sunshine, reflecting all the shades of purple, mauve and lilac around the room.

Perhaps everyone had the same idea, but it was Lily who said, "I think these are presents for us from our dragons."

"And I think that they've gone," her brother added glumly.

Minnie said, "They are off on their adventures," making the children feel less sad.

"And I believe that these gifts are to thank you both for your friendship," Arthur told them, making them feel better still.

"Thank you," Lily and Alexander called together to the absent dragons.

"Maybe we will see them here again one day," Minnie said and they all fell into a comfortable group hug.

"Farewell dear dragons!" muttered Arthur.

"Stay safe!" added Minnie.

"Goodbye and good luck, dragons," the children murmured together, hoping that somehow the dragons would understand.

Epilogue

The children's dragon times had come to an end. Good times, as well as bad times, usually do.

And so it was with the virus. Eventually Lily and Alexander were able to return home to their mum, their friends and their school.

Some things were different, but many of the good things were the same.

Their mum was amazed when she heard all about the dragons. She was even more amazed when Lily and Alexander gave her the little purple gemstone. It fetched a marvellous price in a big auction and they had enough money for a fantastic holiday and to have a little hen coop built in their garden for their three new chickens!

The children had given the emerald to Minnie and Arthur. They sold it and were then able to fund the necessary repairs to Bixham Hall. Alexander and Lily remained in close contact with the elderly couple and visited them in the school holidays.

None of them ever saw a dragon again, but hope remains that they will, one day.

Dragon Times - suggestions for your own illustrations

Zelda   Hint - Chapters 6 & 8
Sparky   Hint - Chapter 10
Lily   Hint - Chapter 1
Alexander   Hint - Chapter 2
Mum   Hint - Chapter 2
Minnie   Hint - Chapter 2
Arthur   Hint - Chapter 4
Bixham Hall   Hint - Chapter 2
Castle   Hint - Chapters 5 & 15
Hen coop &/or hens   Hint - Chapter 4
Fish pond   Hint - Chapter 4
Summerhouse   Hint - Chapter 4
Orchard   Hint - Chapter 10
Lake &/or heron   Hint - Chapter 16
Emerald & gemstone   Hint - Chapter 18

How about drawing your own plan of the rear gardens? Remember to include the features listed above, plus the kitchen garden, the rose garden, the knot garden, the stile & fence, the meadow, the copse, the brook with its stepping stones, the clearing and the topiary avenue with the bridge over the stream leading to the lake.

What did Lily and Alexander learn during these strange times?

Make a list *before* looking at these children's ideas!

Ideas from some readers – do you agree? Can you think of any more?

- Resilience – don't give up & keep trying
- Home grown food tastes better
- Appreciate your family – love your brothers and sisters!
- Look after nature
- Gardening
- Recycle water & avoid waste
- Simple things are fun (exploring, finding recipes, cooking)
- How to look after hens & bird watching
- Community –help and look after other people
- Count your blessings

<u>* What did you learn in these strange times?</u>

<u>How about designing your own dragon?</u>

- What does he or she look like?
- What would you call your dragon?
- Where does he or she live?
- Can your dragon fly or breathe fire?
- Does he or she have any other special powers?